P9-BYK-163

A Glow-in-the-Dark Encounter

WRITTEN AND ILLUSTRATED BY

Dr. Seuss

RANDOM HOUSE  NEW YORK

TM & copyright © by Dr. Seuss Enterprises, L.P. 1961, renewed 1989.

All rights reserved.
Published in the United States by Random House Children's Books,
a division of Random House, Inc., 1745 Broadway, New York, NY, 10019.
"What Was I Scared Of?" was originally published in a slightly different form
as part of *The Sneetches and Other Stories,* published by Random House Children's Books,
a division of Random House, Inc., New York, in 1961.

Random House and colophon are registered trademarks of Random House, Inc.

Visit us on the Web!
www.randomhouse.com/kids
www.seussville.com

Educators and librarians, for a variety of teaching tools, visit us at www.randomhouse.com/teachers

Library of Congress Cataloging-in-Publication Data
Seuss, Dr. What was I scared of? : a glow-in-the-dark encounter / [by Dr. Seuss]. — Glow-in-the-dark ed.
p. cm.
Summary: The narrator is frightened by a pair of pale green pants with no one inside
that seems to be following him, until the two meet and discover that they have nothing to fear.
Features illustrations that glow in the dark.
ISBN 978-0-375-85342-5 (trade) — ISBN 978-0-375-95867-0 (lib. bdg.)
1. Glow-in-the-dark books—Specimens. [1. Stories in rhyme. 2. Fear—Fiction.
3. Glow-in-the-dark books. 4. Toy and movable books.] I. Title.
PZ8.3.G276Wh 2009
[E]—dc22
2008021879

MANUFACTURED IN CHINA
20 19 18 17 16 15 14 13 12
First Glow-in-the-Dark Edition

Random House Children's Books supports the First Amendment and celebrates the right to read.

W_{ell} . . .
I was walking in the night
And I saw nothing scary.
For I have never been afraid
Of anything. Not very.

Then I was deep within the woods
When, suddenly, I spied them.
I saw a pair of pale green pants
With nobody inside them!

I wasn't scared. But, yet, I stopped.
What *could* those pants be there for?
What *could* a pair of pants at night
Be standing in the air for?

And then they moved! Those empty pants!
They kind of started jumping.
And then my heart, I must admit,
It kind of started thumping.

So I got out. I got out fast
As fast as I could go, sir.
I wasn't scared. But pants like that
I did not care for. No, sir.

After that, a week went by.
Then one dark night in Grin-itch
(I had to do an errand there
And fetch some Grin-itch spinach) . . .
Well, I had fetched the spinach.
I was starting back through town
When those pants raced round a corner
And they almost knocked me down!

I lost my Grin-itch spinach
But I didn't even care.
I ran for home! Believe me,
I had really had a scare!

Now, bicycles were never made
For pale green pants to ride 'em,
Especially spooky pale green pants
With nobody inside 'em!

And the NEXT night, I was fishing
For Doubt-trout on Roover River
When those pants came rowing toward me!
Well, I started in to shiver.

And by now I was SO frightened
That, I'll tell you, but I hate to . . .
I screamed and rowed away and lost
My hook and line and bait, too!

I ran and found a Brickel bush.
I hid myself away.
I got brickels in my britches
But I stayed there anyway.

I stayed all night. The next night, too.

I'd be there still, no doubt,

But I had to do an errand

So, the *next* night, I went out.

I had to do an errand,
Had to pick a peck of Snide
In a dark and gloomy Snide-field
That was almost nine miles wide.

I said, "I do not fear those pants
With nobody inside them."
I said, and said, and said those words.
I said them. But I lied them.

Then I reached inside a Snide bush
And the next thing that I knew,
I felt my hand touch someone!
And I'll bet that you know who.

And there I was! Caught in the Snide!
And in that dreadful place
Those spooky, empty pants and I
Were standing face to face!

I yelled for help. I screamed. I shrieked.
I howled. I yowled. I cried,
"Oh, save me from these pale green pants
With nobody inside!"

But then a strange thing happened.
Why, those pants began to cry!
Those pants began to tremble.
They were just as scared as I!

I never heard such whimpering
And I began to see
That I was just as strange to them
As they were strange to me!

I put my arm around their waist
And sat right down beside them.
I calmed them down.
Poor empty pants
With nobody inside them.

And, now, we meet quite often,
Those empty pants and I,
And we never shake or tremble.
We both smile
And we say
"Hi!"

Hi!